A Note to Parents

Welcome to REAL KIDS READERS, a series of phonics-based books for children who are beginning to read. In the classroom, educators use phonics to teach children how to sound out unfamiliar words, providing a firm foundation for reading skills. At home, you can use REAL KIDS READERS to reinforce and build on that foundation, because the books follow the same basic phonic guidelines that children learn in school.

Of course the best way to help your child become a good reader is to make the experience fun—and REAL KIDS READERS do that, too. With their realistic story lines and lively characters, the books engage children's imaginations. With their clean design and sparkling photographs, they provide picture clues that help new readers decipher the text. The combination is sure to entertain young children and make them truly want to read.

REAL KIDS READERS have been developed at three distinct levels to make it easy for children to read at their own pace.

- LEVEL 1 is for children who are just beginning to read.
- LEVEL 2 is for children who can read with help.
- LEVEL 3 is for children who can read on their own.

A controlled vocabulary provides the framework at each level. Repetition, rhyme, and humor help increase word skills. Because children can understand the words and follow the stories, they quickly develop confidence. They go back to each book again and again, increasing their proficiency and sense of accomplishment, until they're ready to move on to the next level. The result is a rich and rewarding experience that will help them develop a lifelong love of reading.

For Dan Weiss,
of course
–M. L.

Special thanks to
L.L. Bean, Inc., Freeport, Maine,
for supplying clothing and equipment.

Produced by DWAI / Seventeenth Street Productions, Inc.

Library of Congress Cataloging-in-Publication Data

Leonard, Marcia.
    Dan and Dan / by Marcia Leonard ; photography by Dorothy Handelman.
        p.   cm. — (Real kids readers. Level 1)
    Summary: Dan describes the things he does with his grandfather who is also named Dan.
    ISBN 0-7613-2003-2 (lib. bdg.). — ISBN 0-7613-2028-8 (pbk.)
    [1. Grandfathers—Fiction. 2. Stories in rhyme.] I. Handelman, Dorothy, ill. II. Title.
III. Series.
PZ8.3.L54925Daj   1998
[E]—dc21
                                                                                        97-31375
                                                                                        CIP
                                                                                        AC

pbk: 10 9 8 7 6 5 4
lib: 10 9 8 7 6 5 4

Dan and Dan

Marcia Leonard

Photographs by **Dorothy Handelman**

M

The Millbrook Press

Brookfield, Connecticut

You are Dan.
I am Dan too.

5

But I am not
the same as you.

I am a kid.

9

You are a man.

11

I can not wink.
But you can, Dan.

I like milk cold.
You like it hot.

You take a nap.
But I do not.

You like to sit.

I like to run.

21

But we still have
a lot of fun.

We sing. We swim.
We play with pets.

We hunt for bugs
with our bug nets.

We go on trips
in your big van.

You are my dad's dad,
and I love you, Dan.

Reading with Your Child

1. Try to read with your child at least twenty minutes each day, as part of your regular routine.
2. Keep your child's books in one convenient, cozy reading spot.
3. Read and familiarize yourself with the Phonic Guidelines below.
4. Ask your child to read *Dan and Dan* out loud. If he or she has difficulty with a word:
   - Help him or her decode the word phonetically. (Say, "Try to sound it out.")
   - Encourage him or her to use picture clues. (Say, "What does the picture show?")
   - Ask him or her to use context clues. (Say, "What would make sense?")
5. If your child still doesn't "get" the word, tell him or her what it is. Don't wait for frustration to build.
6. Praise your beginning reader. With your enthusiasm and encouragement, your child will go from one success to the next.

Phonic Guidelines

Use the following guidelines to help your child read the words in *Dan and Dan*.

Short Vowels
When two consonants surround a vowel, the sound of the vowel is usually short. This means you pronounce *a* as in apple, *e* as in egg, *i* as in igloo, *o* as in octopus, and *u* as in umbrella. Short-vowel words in this story include: *big, bug, but, can, dad, Dan, fun, hot, kid, lot, man, nap, nets, not, pets, run, sit, van.*

Short-Vowel Words with Beginning Consonant Blends
When two different consonants begin a word, they usually blend to make a combined sound. Words in this story with beginning consonant blends include: *swim, trips.*

Short-Vowel Words with Ending Consonant Blends
When two different consonants end a word, they usually blend to make a combined sound. Words in this story with ending consonant blends include: *hunt, milk, sing, wink.*

Double Consonants
When two identical consonants appear side by side, one of them is silent. Double-consonant words in this story include: *still.*

Sight Words
Sight words are those words that a reader must learn to recognize immediately—by sight—instead of by sounding them out. They occur with high frequency in easy texts. Sight words not included in the above categories are: *a, am, and, are, as, do, for, go, have, I, in, it, like, love, my, of, on, our, play, same, take, the, to, too, we, with, you, your.*

Plurals
When a noun becomes plural, an *s* or *es* is added. Plural words in this story include: *bugs, nets, pets, trips.*